THE
Cold Water Witch

by Yannick Murphy

Illustrations by Tom Lintern

TRICYCLE PRESS
Berkeley

www.randomhouse.com/kids

Tricycle Press and the Tricycle Press colophon are registered trademarks of Random House, Inc.

Library of Congress Cataloging-in-Publication Data

Murphy, Yannick.
  The Cold Water Witch / by Yannick Murphy ; illustrations by Tom Lintern. -- 1st ed.
    p. cm.
[1. On the coldest winter night, the Cold Water Witch tries to trick a little girl into taking her
place as ruler of the frozen lands, but the little girl fights back. 2. Witches--Fiction. 3. Cold--Fiction.]
I. Lintern, Tom, ill. II. Title.
  PZ7.M9566Co 2010
  [E]--dc22
                                    2009041862

ISBN 978-1-58246-330-8 (hardcover)
ISBN 978-1-58246-356-8 (Gibraltar lib. bdg.)

Printed in China

Design by Judythe Sieck
Typeset in Celestia Antiqua and Nicolas Cochin Antique
The illustrations in this book were created in pencil then edited using Photoshop.

1 2 3 4 5 6 — 15 14 13 12 11 10

First Edition

For Hank, Louisa, and Kit. —Y. M.

For my sisters Jenn and Julia. —T. L.

She came out on the coldest night.

Her fingers were icicles.

She had snow for her hair.

She was looking for a girl.

"Wooooooooo!" she called.
"Little girl, wake up.

Come with me to where the waters run cold.
Come with me to where the world is covered in snow."

"It's the middle of the night. I'm not going anywhere!"
the little girl said.

"WOOOOOOo. Come with me and play. You will
like it there. Let me show you," she said to the little girl.

She blew a cold breath on the window, and with the
tip of her icicle finger she began to draw.

"We will skate across these frozen lakes. We will dash
beneath the falling snow."

"I am a princess there, and you can be one too. You can have a crown made of ice, like mine," she said, and held it out to the girl.

The girl reached for the sparkling crown, but then stopped herself.

The crown's frozen points were as sharp as splintered glass.

"You can't fool me! That's not a crown for a princess," said the girl.

"If you do not believe me," she said to the girl, "then touch my beautiful gown."

The girl did it. She touched the snow-white gown.

"My hand—it's stuck! You're not a princess," the girl cried.

"You are right. I am the Cold Water Witch, and I have caught you!" the witch said. "Now where is your icebox?"

"My icebox? You mean the freezer?" the girl said.

"Yes. Once I put you in it, you will be swept off to the frozen land," said the witch.

"You'll have to drag me," the girl said.

In the kitchen, the witch asked, "Which one is the icebox?"

"There," the girl said, pointing.

The witch opened the door.

It was warm.

It smelled like fresh-baked bread.

"That is not the icebox," hissed the witch.

"Okay, you're right. This is it," the girl said, pointing.

The witch opened another door.

Hot steam sailed out from in between the plates.

"Stop trying to fool me!" cried the witch.

"All right," said the girl. "I give up. You're too smart. Here it is. Maybe I'll like living in the frozen land."

The girl pointed to the freezer.

The Cold Water Witch opened it.

She breathed in the chilly air.

"Ah, yes," she said. "I feel the awful cold. It is time for you to go. Climb inside."

The girl peered into the freezer.
"Wait a second, what's that?" she asked.
"What is what?" said the witch.
"I think I see a beach. I can feel the sun.
It's so warm in here!" said the girl.

"Warm?" asked the witch.

"Ahhh," the girl sighed. "I smell coconut. I hear waves. Are you sure you're sending me to the frozen land? Will I still get an icy crown?"

The Cold Water Witch stuck her head into the freezer.

"Where, where is the beach?" she demanded.

"It's way in the back, behind the frozen peas. Get inside. You'll see it," the girl said.

The witch put one foot into the freezer. She bent down low.

"I still cannot see it!" said the witch.

"You're not in far enough," said the girl.

The witch leaned in more.

"And now I've caught *you!*" said the girl.

From deep inside the freezer, the witch cried, "It is so cold, so very cold."

"But you like the cold," said the girl.

"Oh, no, I do not. I do not want to go back. I never wanted to go in the first place. WooOOOOOo," moaned the witch, but it was a faraway sound, almost like the sound the freezer always made.

"But weren't you always the Cold Water Witch?" asked the girl.

"No. Long ago, on the coldest night, the old Cold Water Witch came for me, just as I came for you," sobbed the witch.

The witch's tears were ice and hard as diamonds. They even bounced when they hit the floor.

"Don't cry," the girl said, and she reached out and touched the witch's snowy hair. The snow began to melt.

"Your hair is brown, like mine!" said the girl. "Are there others like you in the frozen land?"

"No," sighed the witch. "It is so lonely there."

The girl helped the witch climb out of the freezer.

The witch's fingers were no longer icicles. They were as warm as the girl's. And the witch's tears fell like real tears, silently onto the floor.

"I have to go back. Someone has to rule the land," said the witch, and she turned to the freezer door.

"But look at you now," the girl said, standing the witch in front of the glass oven door.

The witch gasped. "I'm me again!"

Her voice, which once howled "Wooooooooo" like the winter wind, was now soft and warm.

"Don't go back!" said the girl. "No one's there to care. Stay with me. Come on!"

Together they skipped back to the girl's bedroom.

They used blankets and made a playhouse tent.
They sipped tea from small china cups.

They folded paper fans and made believe
they were at a white sandy beach.

And even though it was the coldest night, they said, "Oh my, this heat!" and fanned each other and laughed under an imaginary summer sun.